Keeping up with the Pomeranians
SUSAN MARIE CHAPMAN
I0843655

Published 2025

Printed in the United States of America
Print ISBN: 978-1-966895-51-0

Canoe Tree Books is an imprint of DartFrog Books
Charlotte, NC
www.DartFrogBooks.com

Dedicated to Situ Bruce-K.
The heartbeat of Miami Beach

A special thanks to Maggy
and Omar at Tropicolor

Sugar and Cookie Chapman live in Miami Beach, Florida. The island of the rich and famous, where fast cars, loud music, and beautiful bodies are the norm.

It is the city of the Versace Mansion, Art Basel and the Fontainbleau Miami Beach Hotel. It is a world-renowned city that never sleeps.

This is where Sugar and Cookie have lived their whole lives. These twin sisters are living *la vida loca* (the crazy life). They do not skip a beat as they glide through the city. They shop, they exercise, they schedule spa days, eat healthily, and repeat.

They also enjoy people-watching on Ocean Drive, a Miami Beach favorite pastime.

Sugar and Cookie are fashion model icons. The fact that they are the most sought after girls in all of Miami Beach does not affect their perfectly demure manner.

Living in Miami is never easy, but keeping up with these two precious Pomeranians is no small task. See if you can keep up with the Pomeranians.

Sugar and Cookie live in Miami Beach.

NICE

Where fast cars,

loud music,

and beautiful bodies
are the norm.

MonEY
&
SIX

It is the city of
Art Basel,

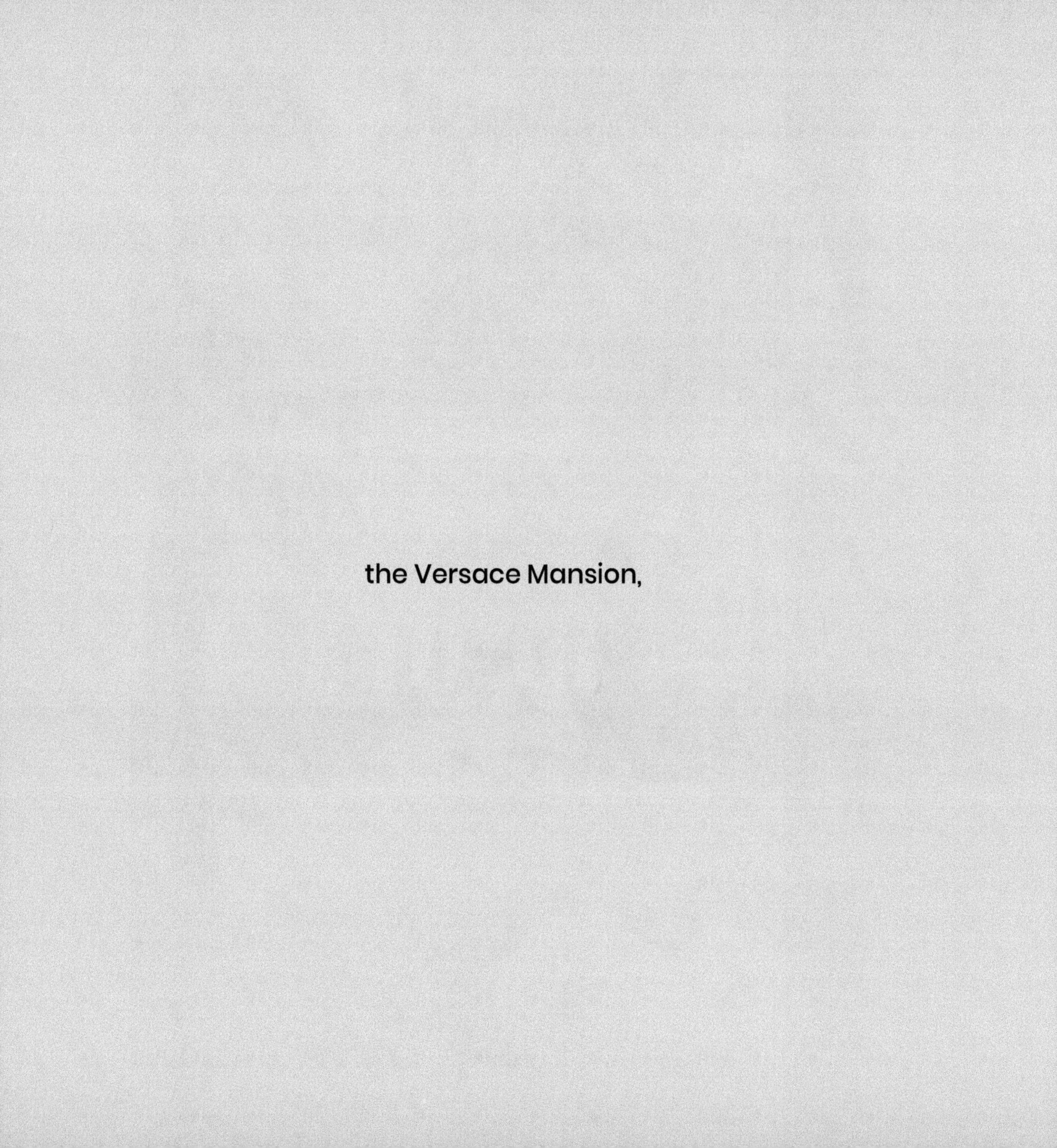

the Versace Mansion,

and the iconic Fontainbleau Miami Beach Hotel.

This is our town

Sugar
Cookie

Sassy and Classy
Can you guess which one is which?

Of course we love boating.
We are in Miami, darling!

LIV
NFL
SUPER BOWL

When special events come to town,
you can be certain that we will be making an appearance.

We are constantly on the go.
No time to waste.

Gen7Pets

Hot guy sighting.

AMI B ACH

Working out is not hard to do in Miami Beach.
Look at all those tight bodies.

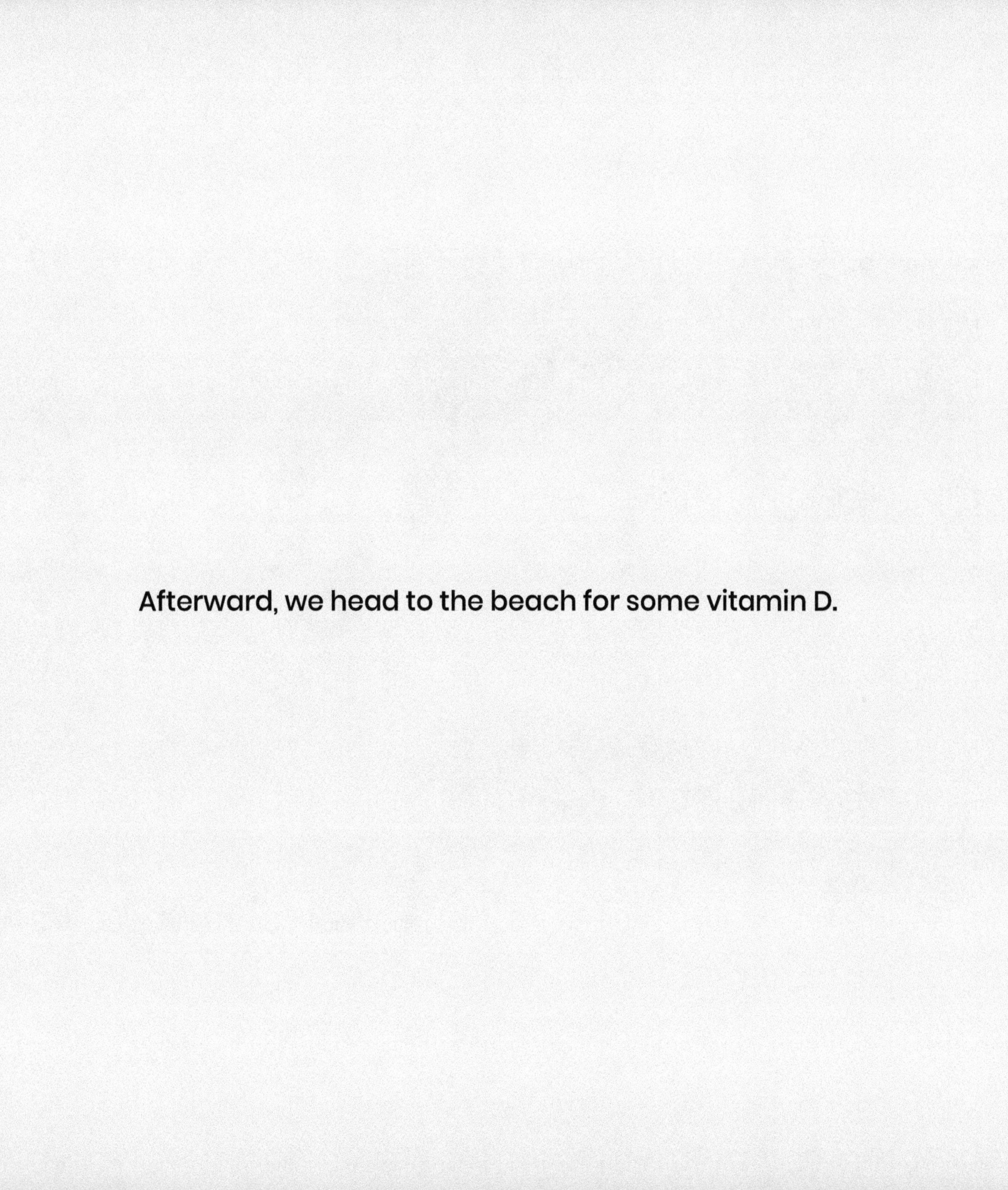

Afterward, we head to the beach for some vitamin D.

Spa Day.
Always be prepared.
You never know when the next soiree will present itself.

Can you say,
"Mani/pedi"?

ORDER ON THE APP
RA VIDA MIAMI
PURA VIDA

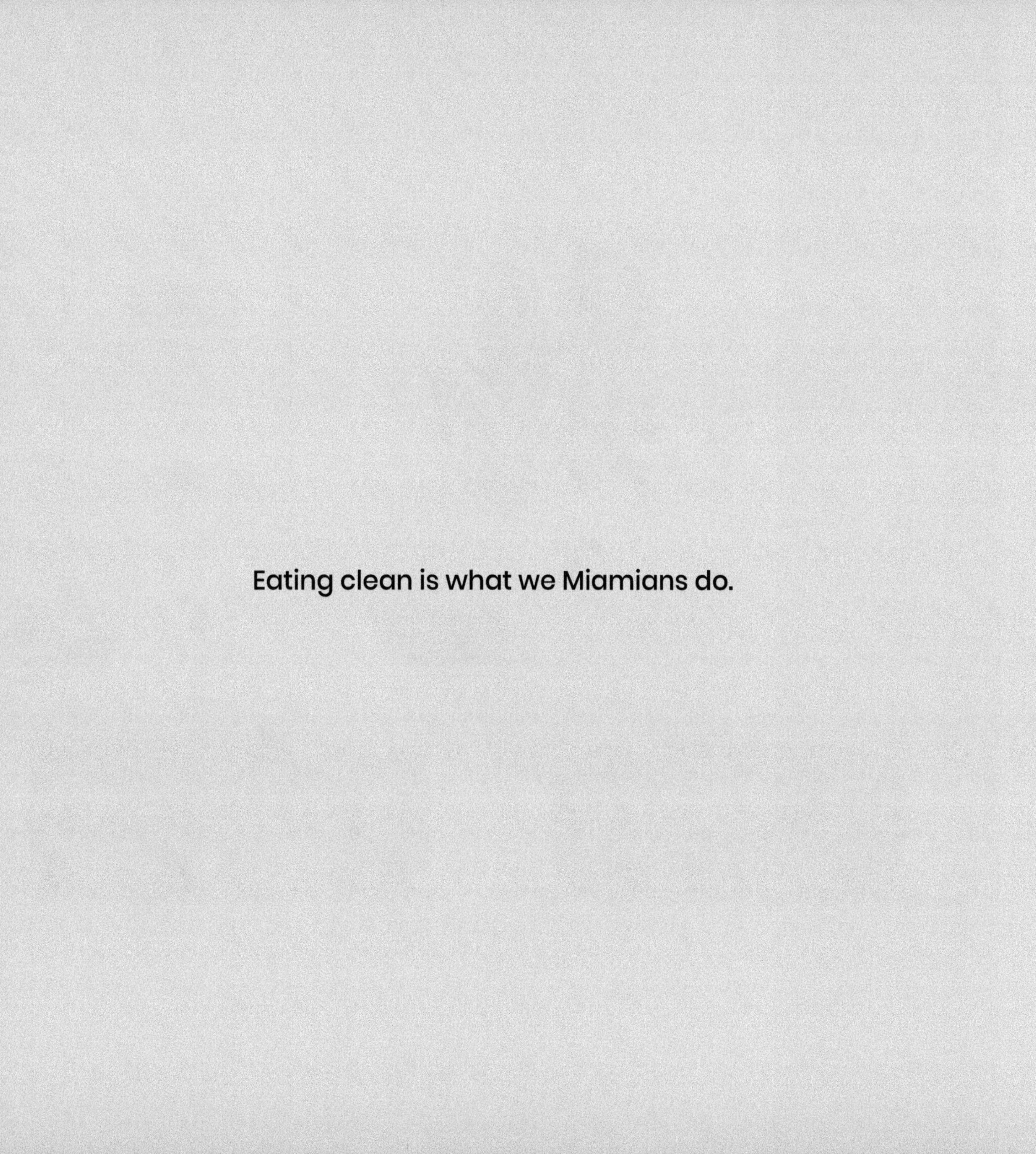

Eating clean is what we Miamians do.

A day of shopping at Bal Harbour Shops,
with a late lunch at Carpaccio's to follow.
Now, that's what I call a perfect Miami day.

Every girl needs a bodyguard, at least once.

PALACE
ACCESSIBLE
ROUTE

Late nights are spent on Ocean Drive, always at the Palace.
And always with our favorite Drag Queen.

Keeping up with the Pomeranians
is hard to do.
But, you can
at least try.

XO

Sugar & Cookie

www.ingramcontent.com/pod-product-compliance
Lightning Source LLC
Chambersburg PA
CBHW041148300726
48978CB00017B/1432